PINOCCHIO

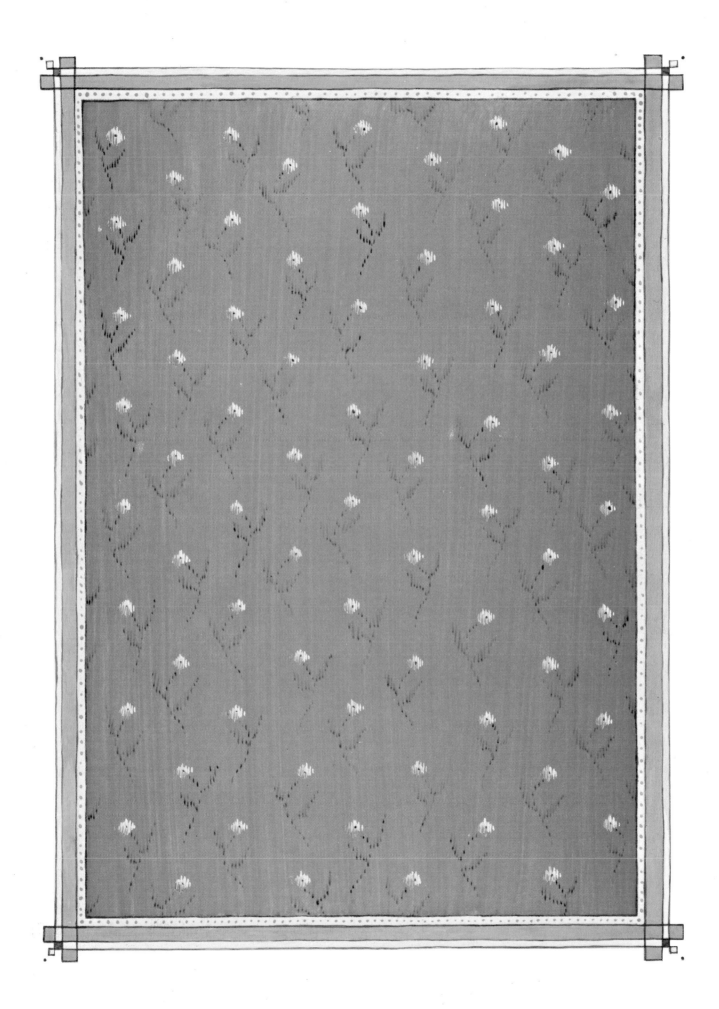

The Adventures of

BY CARLO COLLODI
ILLUSTRATED BY DIANE GOODE
Adapted by Stephanie Spinner

A LOOKING GLASS LIBRARY BOOK

Random House New York

Library of Congress Cataloging in Publication Data: Spinner, Stephanie. The adventures of Pinocchio. (Looking glass library)
SUMMARY: A wooden puppet undergoes many trials and tribulations because of his mischievousness and disobedience. [1. Fairy
tales. 2. Puppets—Fiction] I. Goode, Diane, ill. II. Collodi, Carlo, 1826–1890. Avventure di Pinocchio. III.
Title. PZ8.S465Ad 1983 [Fic] 82-24053 ISBN: 0-394-85910-3 (trade); 0-394-95910-8 (lib. bdg.)

There was once an old woodcarver named Geppetto who lived in a country far across the sea. He often longed for a companion, so one day he decided to carve himself a puppet—a little wooden boy. After pulling out his tools and a fine log of wood, he quickly got to work, thinking, as he carved, about all the things he and his new puppet would do together. The puppet would sing and dance and turn somersaults. Geppetto would travel with him from town to town, enjoying the sights. They would have one good time after another. But best of all, the puppet would be like his very own son. "I think I'll call him Pinocchio," the old man decided. "The name has a lucky sound to it."

Geppetto had carved Pinocchio's hair and forehead and was starting on his nose when a very strange thing happened. Though he kept trying to whittle it down to size, the puppet's nose grew and grew, as if it had a life all its own. And when Geppetto carved its mouth, the puppet rolled its eyes and then stuck out its tongue! "This little fellow is unruly," thought Geppetto. "He's going to have to learn some manners!" But he said nothing and kept carving until Pinocchio was finished.

Then he stood the puppet on the floor to teach him how to walk. At first Pinocchio had difficulty, because his wooden legs were stiff. But soon he got the hang of it and was skipping gaily around the cottage while Geppetto cried out, "Good, very good!" Then, as the old man looked on in bewilderment, the puppet danced right past him, darted through the open door, and scampered down the street. He was running away!

Geppetto hobbled after his puppet as quickly as he could, but Pinocchio was much too fast for him. Down the street he raced while Geppetto cried, "Stop him! Stop him, someone, please!" But no one could. Even the policeman who grabbed Pinocchio by his long nose could not hold on to him. With a mischievous smile the puppet wriggled free and ran back to Geppetto's cottage. Once he was certain that he was alone, he locked the door and flung himself into a chair, quite pleased with his escape.

Suddenly he heard a sharp little sound: "Cri-cri-cri!"

"Who's there?" called Pinocchio, frightened.

"I am!" said a voice. Pinocchio turned around and saw a big Cricket crawling slowly up the wall.

"And who are you?" asked Pinocchio.

"I am the Talking Cricket, and I have lived in this room for a hundred years."

"This room is mine now," said Pinocchio rudely. "Go away!"

"Before I go, allow me to tell you something," said the Cricket. "Woe to boys who do not obey their parents and run away from home. They will never be happy."

"Be quiet!" said Pinocchio. "I'm not like other boys, and I don't want to be. What's more, I won't go to school and be forced to study. Tomorrow I'm leaving this place forever. I'm going to chase butterflies, climb trees, and wander around from morning till night."

"Do that, and you will grow up to be a donkey."

"Careful, Cricket," said Pinocchio. "If you make me angry, you'll be sorry."

"*I* am sorry for *you*," said the Cricket.

"Why?"

"Because you are a puppet—you silly woodenhead!"

When he heard this, Pinocchio jumped up angrily and threw a wooden hammer straight at the Cricket. With a feeble "cri-cri-cri," the Cricket fell from the wall and crawled away.

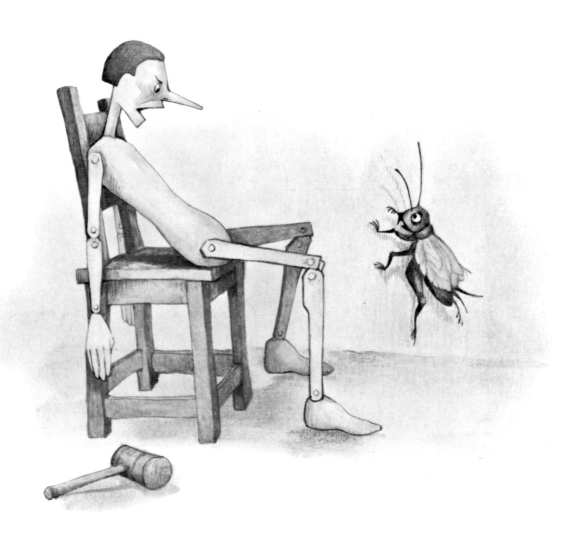

Pinocchio was sorry, but not for long.

As the afternoon passed, all he could think about was how hungry he was. He hadn't eaten anything all day, and now it was beginning to grow dark.

"Oh," he wailed, "the Talking Cricket was right! If only I'd been good and not run away from my papa, he would be here right now with something for me to eat. How horrible it is to be hungry!"

Wishing that he had anything—a piece of bread, a dry crust, even an old bone to chew on—he searched everywhere in Geppetto's tiny cottage. But he found nothing. So he decided to go out into the village to beg for food.

The night was pitch black and the streets were deserted. The whole town was asleep. But Pinocchio was desperate. He went to the nearest house and rang the doorbell, which pealed loudly in the quiet. "That will bring somebody," thought Pinocchio.

And so it did. A little man in a nightcap appeared in the window and called down angrily, "Just what do you want?"

"A piece of bread," called Pinocchio. "I'm so hungry."

"Wait there. I'll be right back," said the man, who thought Pinocchio was one of those bad boys who liked to ring doorbells at night just for fun. After a minute he called from the window, "Come underneath here and hold out your hands."

Pinocchio rushed under the window. He got there just in time to be drenched by a bucket of ice-cold water! The old man slammed the window shut, and poor, wet Pinocchio walked back to Geppetto's cottage in the dark.

Hungry, cold, and very unhappy, the puppet sat down with his feet on the stove and soon fell asleep.

He was awakened by the sound of Geppetto coming home the next morning. Pinocchio jumped up to greet him and then fell clattering to the floor. His wooden feet had burned away on the stove while he slept!

When Geppetto saw what had happened to his puppet, he was so

overcome with pity
that he forgot to
scold Pinocchio for
running away. Instead he
picked him up and caressed him.
"Little one, how did you burn
your feet?" he asked.

Pinocchio told him everything that
had happened the night before—how
the Talking Cricket had called him a
woodenhead, how he had gone out
begging for food in the dark and
gotten doused with a bucket of
freezing water, and how he had gone
to sleep on the stove and woken up
without his feet! All in all it was such
a sad story that Pinocchio was
wailing and crying by the time he
finished it.

Geppetto shook his head
sympathetically. "I could make you
new feet," he said. "But if I did,
you'd run away again, wouldn't
you?"

"I won't," said Pinocchio. "I promise."

"And will you go to school, like a
good boy?"

"I will," answered the puppet.

So Geppetto got out his tools and
two small pieces of well-seasoned

wood and set to work. In less than an hour the feet were finished. Then Geppetto glued the feet to Pinocchio's legs. As soon as they were attached Pinocchio leaped up and danced around the room. "Thank you, thank you!" he cried. "I'm so grateful to you, Papa!"

"Now you are ready to go to school," said the old woodcarver.

A little gleam of mischief came into Pinocchio's eyes. "But how can I go to school without any clothes?" he asked innocently.

"Hmmm. I hadn't thought of that," said Geppetto, who had no money at all to buy clothes for Pinocchio. "I suppose I'll have to make you some." And in no time Pinocchio was dressed in a gaily colored suit of flowered paper and a lumpy little cap made out of dough.

Pinocchio ran to look at himself in a basin of water. "I look like a gentleman!" he said, twirling around.

"So you do," said Geppetto. "Now off to school you go."

"I can't go, Papa. There's something else I need."

"What is that?"

"A spelling book."

Geppetto sighed. "I cannot buy you one, for my pockets are empty."

"Then I can't go to school after all." Pinocchio tried to look sad, but he was secretly pleased.

Geppetto said nothing. Instead he took his coat and left the cottage. When he came back a while later, he no longer had his coat, even though it was snowing outside.

"Where's your coat, Papa?" asked Pinocchio.

"It was too warm for me, so I sold it," said Geppetto. Then he handed Pinocchio a brand-new spelling book.

Pinocchio realized that Geppetto had sold his coat to buy him the book. He threw himself into the old man's arms and kissed him again and again. "I'll go to school right now," he declared. "I'm going to make you proud of me." And off he went, his heart full of good intentions.

Pinocchio had not walked far when he heard the sound of flutes and drums playing in the distance. "I'll go to school later," he thought. Following the music, he came to a crowd milling about in front of a large tent. There was a brightly painted sign over the entranceway, and Pinocchio could hear waves of laughter coming from inside.

He turned to a boy standing nearby. "What does the sign say?" he asked.

"Puppet Theater," answered the boy. "Don't you have money for a ticket?"

Pinocchio had never seen a puppet show and he dearly wanted to. "How much is a ticket?" he asked.

"Four pennies," said the boy, edging toward the entrance.

"Wait!" said Pinocchio. "Can you lend me the money? I have none."

"I don't lend money," said the boy matter-of-factly.

"Then how about buying my new spelling book?" Pinocchio asked. "I'll sell it to you for four cents."

"No thanks," said the boy, "I've got one." With this he walked into the tent, and Pinocchio's heart sank.

"I'll buy your book," said a peddler in the crowd.

Pinocchio handed over his book, grabbed the money, and dashed into the theater. He would go to school some other day!

Once inside, Pinocchio found the dancing and the singing of the puppets so exciting that he leaped onstage to be with them. The puppets greeted Pinocchio like a long-lost brother, shouting his name with joy and lifting him onto their shoulders as they cavorted around the stage. At first the audience thought this was funny, but after a few minutes they began to shout at the puppets to continue their play. The puppets paid no attention—until there was a monstrous growl and the horrible crack of a whip, and Fire Eater the Puppet Master appeared.

"What is the meaning of this?" he shouted. "And who are you?" he demanded of Pinocchio. Fire Eater was a giant of a man with a huge mouth, a long black beard, and eyes that seemed to burn with an angry red flame. Before Pinocchio could answer, Fire Eater cracked his whip again and all the puppets jumped back in terror.

"Continue the play," he growled. "I will take care of you later."

As soon as the play was over, Fire Eater called for Pinocchio to be brought to him. "The fire cooking my dinner is not hot enough!" he shouted. "Let's throw this rascal onto the flames. He's made of good hard wood—he'll make the fire burn brightly!"

When Pinocchio heard this, he cried for mercy with tears pouring

down his cheeks. Fire Eater watched him without saying a word. Then he sneezed loudly and blew his nose.

"That's a good sign," whispered one of the puppets carrying Pinocchio. "It means he feels sorry for you." And it was true. Through his tears Pinocchio could see that Fire Eater really was crying, and in between sobs he was sneezing over and over, as if he had a terrible cold.

At last Fire Eater managed to say, "Stop crying! You're making me feel very strange indeed," and with that he sneezed three times.

"God bless you!" said Pinocchio.

"Thanks!" said Fire Eater, calming down a little. "Now tell me, do you have a father and a mother?"

"I have a wonderful, kind father named Geppetto," said Pinocchio, "who sold his only coat to buy me a spelling book."

Fire Eater started sneezing again. "Poor man! Think how sad he would have been if I had thrown you into the fire! Oh, how sorry I am for him," and he sneezed four times.

"God bless you again!" said Pinocchio.

Fire Eater groped around in his pocket for his handkerchief. When he pulled it out, he had five gold coins in his hand also. "Give these to Geppetto so he can buy himself another coat," he said.

Pinocchio was so grateful that he threw himself onto Fire Eater's lap and kissed him right on the nose.

"Go now," said Fire Eater, sneezing thunderously, "or I may change my mind about you."

Pinocchio called good-bye to all the puppets and scampered out of the theater, the gold coins jingling merrily in his pocket.

Just as he was thinking about the gold coat with diamond buttons that he would buy Geppetto, he was greeted by a lame Fox and a blind Cat who were helping each other down the road.

"Good afternoon, Pinocchio," said the Fox with a sly smile.

"How do you know my name?" asked Pinocchio in surprise.

"I know your father, Geppetto," said the Fox. "He has been look-

ing for you everywhere, poor man, without a coat to warm him
against the cold."

"He will have a fine new coat very soon," said Pinocchio proudly.
"I'm going to buy him one."

"How will you manage that?" asked the Cat with a snicker.

"With these," said Pinocchio, bringing out the five gold coins that
Fire Eater had given him.

When they saw the coins, the Fox reached out with his lame paw as if to grab them, and the Cat's eyes opened wide, glittering with greed. Before Pinocchio noticed, they quickly pretended to be lame and blind again and the Fox asked smoothly, "What else will you buy with your money?"

"A spelling book," said Pinocchio. "I want to go to school and study hard."

"Tsk, tsk," said the Fox. "It's a good thing you met us, Pinocchio. We can tell you from personal experience—school's a big mistake. Why, wanting to study led to my lameness! And my poor friend here lost his sight from reading too much. You don't want to end up like us, do you?"

Just then a Blackbird sitting on a branch nearby called out, "Pinocchio! Don't listen to bad advice, or you'll be sorry!"

The bird had scarcely finished speaking when the Cat leaped on him and swallowed him up, feathers and all.

"Poor Blackbird!" said Pinocchio. "Why did you do that?"

"To teach him a lesson," said the Cat. "Next time he'll be more careful with his words!"

"As I was saying," continued the Fox, "how lucky it is that we met, Pinocchio. We're going to help you turn your five gold coins into thousands!"

"Thousands!" exclaimed Pinocchio. "How?"

"Simple," said the Fox. "A few miles from here is a magic place called the Field of Wonders. When you bury a gold coin in the Field, water it well, and leave it overnight, the next day you will find that the gold coin has sprouted and grown into a tree! And this tree does not bear leaves or flowers, it bears gold coins!"

"Gold coins!" echoed the Cat longingly.

Pinocchio was amazed to hear this. "If I bury my five gold pieces in the Field, how many will I find the next day?"

The Fox calculated for a moment. "Two thousand five hundred. And just think how happy your father will be."

"So he will!" cried Pinocchio. "When can we go to this wonderful Field?"

"We'll set out at midnight," said the Fox. "Until then, let's stop at the Inn of the Red Lobster for something to eat."

Pinocchio forgot about going home and going to school, and followed his new companions happily. He was so excited by thoughts of the gold-bearing tree that he could eat nothing but a crust of bread and a few walnuts. The Fox said he wasn't very hungry either and ate a simple meal—one rabbit, a dozen chickens, some partridges, a few pheasants, and a side order of frogs and lizards.

The Cat announced that he was too weak to eat much. He could only finish thirty-five small fish in tomato sauce and four helpings of tripe with extra butter and cheese.

With a stomachache from thinking of gold coins, Pinocchio went to sleep in the room the Fox had ordered for him. No sooner had he closed his eyes than he began to dream of a tree in a grassy field. The tree sparkled and glittered, for thousands of gold coins hung from its branches. The coins tinkled softly, as if they were saying, "Whoever wants us must come and get us."

Pinocchio was stretching out his hand to pick them when there were three loud knocks on his door. It was the innkeeper, coming to wake him at midnight.

"Are my companions ready?" asked Pinocchio.

"Ready? They're nowhere to be found," said the innkeeper. "And they didn't pay for their supper either. You'll have to take care of that."

Puzzled by his friends' behavior, Pinocchio paid the innkeeper one of his gold coins and set off for the Field of Wonders on his own.

It was very dark outside and so quiet that the only sound he could hear was his own stumbling footsteps. Then he heard a faint "cri-cri-cri" and saw a dim orange glow in the branches of a large tree.

A moment later a familiar voice said, "Pinocchio, go home at once!" It was the Talking Cricket. "Heed my advice," said the Cricket. "Go back to your father with your four gold pieces. He is deeply unhappy because he thinks you are lost forever."

"Tomorrow my father will be very rich, because those four gold pieces will turn into thousands."

"Listen to me! Do not trust anyone who promises to make you rich overnight! Go back home to your father!"

"Cricket, I have no use for your tiresome advice," said Pinocchio rudely. "Leave me alone."

The Cricket gave a faint sigh. "Then I wish you good luck," he said. "And heaven protect you from thieves this night." With that he disappeared, and the night seemed darker than ever.

Pinocchio stumbled on, feeling more alone than he liked to admit, for by this time he could hardly see his long nose in front of him in the blackness. "Humpf!" he said to himself defiantly. "That Cricket is such a nuisance—always scolding me and telling me what to do. Then when I don't listen, he tries to make me feel bad with all his talk of danger and thieves. Why, I don't believe in thieves! And if one attacked me, I'd just walk up to him and say, 'Listen here, thief! Don't bother me! I'm simply not interested!' "

Just then Pinocchio heard the rustling of leaves behind him. He turned to find two coal-black creatures looming over him like a couple of dark ghosts. The black sacks they wore covered everything but their eyes, which gleamed with a sinister light.

"Thieves!" thought Pinocchio, popping the gold coins into his mouth to hide them. He tried to run, but the two creatures grabbed his arms and hissed, "Your money or your life!"

Because the coins were in his mouth, Pinocchio did not answer. Instead he shook his head imploringly, as if to say that he was only a poor puppet who had no money. But when he did this the coins jingled, and the two creatures cried, "Aha! Open your mouth, you rascal!" When he refused, one creature grabbed his nose, the other grabbed his chin, and together they forced his mouth open. Pinocchio felt a furry cat's paw reaching for the coins and bit down as hard as he could. The creature yowled in pain, and Pinocchio twisted free and ran off at full speed.

Dawn was bright in the sky when Pinocchio, still running, saw a little cottage through the trees. "If only I can reach that cottage, somehow I will be safe," he thought. Running with every last bit of his strength, he came to the cottage and knocked breathlessly on the door.

It was opened by a beautiful Fairy. Her pale skin glowed like moonlight, and her hair was as blue as the summer sky. "What is the trouble?" she asked softly, leading him inside. "Can I help you?"

Pinocchio told her how he had been chased into the forest by two terrible creatures who wanted to steal his gold coins.

"Where are the coins now?" asked the Blue Fairy. "Do you still have them?"

Though the gold coins were in his pocket, Pinocchio lied. "No," he said. "I lost them." No sooner had he said this than his long nose began to grow even longer.

"And where did you lose them?" asked the Fairy.

"In the woods." At this second lie his nose grew longer still.

"Then let us go and find them," said the Fairy in her soft voice.

"No—I forgot!" said Pinocchio. "I didn't lose them, I swallowed

them!" At this third lie his nose grew so long that it reached all the way across the room! Pinocchio moved his head one way and his nose hit the window; he moved it another way and his nose hit the door. The puppet began to shriek and cry in distress. Lying had made his nose so long that he was trapped!

The Fairy watched, saying nothing. When she felt that he had been punished enough, she took pity on him and clapped her hands twice. At this signal a flock of woodpeckers flew in through the window, landed on Pinocchio's nose, and pecked away at it busily. Soon it was down to its normal size.

"What a kind fairy you are," said the puppet gratefully. "Now if you'll allow me to, I'll go home to my father, Geppetto."

"Go then, and be a good boy." The Fairy kissed him, and Pinocchio was on his way.

He had not gone far when a large Pigeon called down to him from the sky, "Hello there! Are you Pinocchio?"

Pinocchio stopped in his tracks. "Yes, I am."

The Pigeon flew down to the ground with a rush of his blue-gray wings. "Then you must know Geppetto," he said.

"He is my father!" cried Pinocchio. "Do you have news of him? Where is he?"

"He is at the seashore building himself a little boat," said the Pigeon. "He plans to sail across the ocean, in hopes of finding you in some foreign land."

"I must go to the seashore!" said Pinocchio. "Is it far from here?"

"Yes, it is, but I will take you. Just climb onto my back and hang on." Pinocchio put his arms around the Pigeon's soft feathery neck and they rose up into the sky. They flew for hours, until the vast green ocean and the shore came into view. As the Pigeon let Pinocchio down, the puppet saw a group of people standing at the shore, shouting and pointing at the choppy, foam-covered waves. Off in the

distance a man in a little wooden boat was waving, as if for help.

"What's going on?" asked Pinocchio.

"Geppetto the carpenter is out there," said a fisherwoman. "He set out today to find his son, and now it looks as if he may sink, for a terrible storm is brewing." The wind was blowing so hard that the woman had to shout to be heard.

"Geppetto!" screamed Pinocchio. "Here I am!" But Geppetto could not hear him. The next moment a huge wave rose over the boat and it disappeared from sight.

The fisherwoman dabbed at her eyes. "Poor man," she said. "There is no saving him now."

"I will save him! I will save him!" cried Pinocchio, leaping into the icy water. With the winds howling and the waves crashing over him, he set out bravely for Geppetto's boat. Luckily his wooden body kept him afloat, and he found that he could swim quickly and well. But though he swam all day and all night on the stormy sea, he could find no trace of Geppetto. By morning he was so tired that he could swim no farther. He saw an island in the distance and struggled toward it wearily, and just when he had lost all hope of reaching it, a large wave lifted him up and dropped him on the shore.

Pinocchio was glad to be on land again, but his first thoughts were for his father. Pacing up and down the sandy beach, he peered out over the vast stretches of water in hopes of catching a glimpse of Geppetto's boat.

But all he saw was a large Dolphin, who smiled politely and wished him good day.

"Hello!" called Pinocchio. "Have you by chance seen my father, Geppetto, out at sea in his little boat?"

"I'm afraid not," replied the Dolphin. "I've seen only you—and that dreadful monster the Dogfish, who terrorizes these waters. If your father was out sailing, the Dogfish has probably swallowed him by now. He's very large, you know, and very ferocious."

Pinocchio was filled with dread. "How large?" he asked.

"As big as a five-story house, with an appetite to match," answered the Dolphin.

At this news Pinocchio began to cry.

"Poor boy!" said the Dolphin. "What will you do now?"

"I don't know. Is there a town nearby?"

"Take the road on your left and follow your nose," said the Dolphin. "It's Busy Bee Town—you can't miss it."

Pinocchio thanked the Dolphin and hurried off down the road. It wasn't long before he came to a busy village, full of people rushing to and fro doing their work. The sight of a woman carrying a big basket of oranges reminded Pinocchio that he was hungry, so he reached into his pocket for his gold coins. But they were gone!

Pinocchio wondered what to do next. Should he ask some kind person for a few pennies so he could buy food? Geppetto had told him that anyone who was strong enough to work should never beg.

Just then a man came along pulling a wooden cart piled high with coal.

"Pardon me, sir," said Pinocchio. "Would you give a penny to a poor starving boy?"

"I'll give you four pennies if you help me pull this cart," said the man.

Pinocchio turned up his nose. "I'm no donkey," he sniffed.

"Then if you're starving, eat a few slices of your pride—and take care not to get a stomachache," said the man, going on his way.

A few minutes later another man came by carrying three large sacks of rice over his shoulder.

"Kind sir," said Pinocchio. "Could you give a poor hungry boy a penny for some food?"

"Carry one of these sacks for me and I'll give you five pennies," said the man.

"But the sacks are heavy. I don't want to tire myself out."

"Then rest and go hungry," said the man, moving on.

All afternoon Pinocchio asked the hardworking people of Busy Bee Town for money, and all afternoon the answer he got was the same: "Shame on you for begging, when you are strong enough to work and earn your money!"

Finally Pinocchio saw a young woman coming down the street. She wore a blue scarf over her hair, and she was carrying two heavy pails of water.

"Will you give me a drink?" Pinocchio asked her.

"Gladly," she answered, setting down her pails.

Pinocchio drank thirstily. "If only getting food could be as easy," he said when he finished.

"Are you hungry?" asked the woman. Pinocchio nodded. "If you carry my pails home for me, I'll give you a slice of home-baked bread," she offered.

Pinocchio hesitated.

"With lots of butter on it."

He still didn't answer.

"And honey on top too."

Pinocchio couldn't resist. "They look very heavy, but I will carry them for you."

Though it was difficult work, and he had to struggle along a dusty road under the hot sun, Pinocchio carried the pails all the way to the woman's house.

When they arrived, she led him into her kitchen, sat him down at the table, and gave him a fine meal of bread, butter, honey, and sugarplums. He was so hungry that he ate everything on the table before he even raised his head. When he did, an amazing sight met his eyes. The young woman had taken off her scarf, and the hair that fell gently to her shoulders was sky-blue. She was the Blue Fairy!

Pinocchio set down his knife and fork with tears of happiness in his eyes. "How I have missed you!" he cried. Then he told her everything that had happened since he had left her little cottage in the woods. When he finished, he confessed something that had been on his mind for a long time. "I'm tired of being a puppet," he said. "I want to be a real boy."

The Blue Fairy smiled, and her kind eyes seemed to look right into Pinocchio's soul. "You will only become a real boy if you deserve it," she said. "You must be good, or you will remain a puppet forever."

"Am I not a good boy now?"

"No!" said the Blue Fairy. "Good boys do what they are told."

"And I never do what anybody tells me."

"Good boys work hard."

"And I never work—I play and roam around."

"Good boys tell the truth."

Pinocchio hung his head. "I lie sometimes."

"And good boys go to school."

"I will go to school too!" he promised. "Nothing will keep me away from it this time!" Then he asked, "Will my father ever find me?"

"If he doesn't, you will find him," said the Blue Fairy. "But you must be good—everything depends on that."

"I'll try," said Pinocchio.

And he did. He went to school bright and early the next day, carrying a book that the Blue Fairy had given him. Though the boys in

his class pulled his nose and called him a woodenhead because he was a puppet, Pinocchio paid careful attention to the teacher and worked hard at his lessons. And when the boys found out that if they pushed Pinocchio too far he would give them a sharp kick in the shins with his pointy wooden feet, they left him alone. After a while everyone could see that he was a serious student who meant to do well in school. The teacher praised him, and Pinocchio began to feel very pleased with himself. "I'm too wise to get into any more trouble," he told the Blue Fairy.

But the next morning, as he was walking to school, Pinocchio was met by a group of his classmates who were all running down the road in great excitement.

"Pinocchio! Have you heard the news?" they cried. "A giant Dogfish, as big as a five-story house, has been seen near the shore!"

"A giant Dogfish!" exclaimed Pinocchio. "Could it be the same one that swallowed my poor father?"

"We're going to see it," said the boys. "Come along with us."

Pinocchio did not want to miss school—but this might be the same Dogfish that had swallowed Geppetto!

"I'll go after school," he said after thinking a moment longer.

"Woodenhead!" cried his classmates. "He's not going to wait all day for you! Come now—you can miss school just this once."

Pinocchio couldn't help himself. He followed his friends down to the beach and looked out over the water eagerly, but there was no fish to be seen.

"Where is he?" cried Pinocchio.

"Maybe he's gone out to lunch," said one of the boys.

"Or maybe he's decided to go home for a nap," said another.

Then they all started giggling. Pinocchio realized they had played a trick on him. "Why did you lie to me?" he asked angrily.

"Because you come to school early and leave late."

"Because you study so hard."

"Because you're such a goody-goody," they said. "And you make us look bad to the teacher."

"What do you want me to do, then?" asked Pinocchio.

"Be more like us," they demanded. "Forget about school and hard work and lessons for a while."

"I'll never do that!" said Pinocchio, and he meant it.

At this one of the boys got so angry with Pinocchio that he began to push him, another started to throw sand in his face, and a third shouted insults and threats at him. Pinocchio fought back fiercely, kicking and punching his attackers so that they scattered. Then one of the boys picked up Pinocchio's heavy arithmetic book and hurled it at him. Pinocchio ducked, and the book hit one of the boys in the head. He fell down heavily, his face in the sand.

The fighting stopped and the boys drew back in fright.

"Is he dead?" asked Pinocchio. No one answered. Instead they ran away, pale with fear, and Pinocchio was left standing over the fallen boy.

He was trying to revive the boy when two Policemen came along. "What are you doing here?" they demanded.

"Trying to help my schoolmate. He's been hurt."

"Indeed he has," said one of the Policemen sternly. "He's been struck in the head! Did you do this?"

"No, sir, I swear I didn't!"

The other Policeman picked up the heavy book lying next to the schoolboy's head. "Is this what hit him?"

"Yes, sir."

"Whose book is it?"

"Mine."

"That settles it! You're the culprit, and you're coming with us!"

They left the fallen schoolboy with some fishermen and marched Pinocchio off toward the police station. Tears of misery slid out of Pinocchio's eyes. He was innocent, yet who would believe him? And worse, they would soon pass the Blue Fairy's cottage. The thought that she would see him in such disgrace pierced his heart like a thorn. He would rather die!

Just then a gust of wind blew Pinocchio's cap from his head. "Will you let me fetch my hat?" he asked.

"Go ahead, but be quick about it."

Pinocchio raced after his cap until he caught it. But instead of putting it on, he placed it between his teeth and ran toward the sea as fast as his wooden legs would carry him. Seeing that it would be hard to catch him, the Policemen set their fastest Dog after him. With the Dog barking fiercely at his heels, Pinocchio ran to the shore and plunged off a steep cliff into the sea. Unwilling to let him escape, the Dog leaped after him, but when it hit the water, it began to splutter and choke. It could not swim.

"Help! Please help!" barked the Dog. "I'm drowning!"

"Go ahead and drown, then," said Pinocchio from a safe distance.

The Dog sank beneath the water with a pitiful yelp. "I beg you," it whimpered when it struggled to the surface, "don't let me die."

And Pinocchio could not. He swam over to the Dog, grabbed it by the tail, and hauled it onto the beach. It lay there gasping while Pinocchio wondered what to do next. Fearing that the Dog or the Policemen might come after him, he plunged back into the sea. He kept close to the shore in hopes that he would find a safe place, and soon spotted a little cave on a rocky beach. He swam toward it and suddenly found himself caught up in a net with thousands of squirming fish. Though he tried, he could not free himself, and he bumped along helplessly as a Fisherman drew the net out of the water and dragged it into the cave.

Inside a fire was burning brightly. By its light Pinocchio could see that the Fisherman was a huge ugly man with watery green eyes and seaweed in his tangled hair. Before the puppet had a chance to say a word, the Fisherman groped around in the net and began to pull out fish one by one. "Fine fish, delicious fish, a good catch today," he said. "Here's mullet, and whitefish, and sole and sardines too." Pinocchio watched as the Fisherman pulled the fish from the net, rolled them in flour, and dropped them into a frying pan that sat on the flames. Then the Fisherman's huge hand reached into the net and closed around Pinocchio. "Now here's a strange fish," he muttered, peering at the puppet with his big green eyes.

"I'm not a fish!" shouted Pinocchio. "I'm a puppet!"

"Hmmm. A puppet fish, eh? Let's see what you taste like," said the Fisherman. "I think I'll fry you."

Pinocchio screamed and cried, wishing with all his heart that he had gone to school that morning instead of listening to his idle friends. But the Fisherman paid him no heed. Instead he rolled him in flour until he was white from head to toe. Just as he was about to drop Pinocchio into the sizzling frying pan with the other fish, a large Dog appeared at the cave, sniffing hungrily. Pinocchio saw that it was the Dog he had saved from drowning.

"Help! Help me or I'll be fried alive!" Pinocchio cried.

The Dog recognized Pinocchio immediately. He leaped at the

Fisherman, snatched Pinocchio away, and shot out of the cave with the puppet in his jaws. When they were far from the Fisherman's cave, the Dog set Pinocchio down on the sand gently and licked the flour from his face.

"Thank you! Oh, thank you!" said Pinocchio.

"You don't have to thank me," said the Dog. "You saved my life first, and I'm glad that I can repay you." Then he offered his paw in friendship and Pinocchio shook it warmly. Wishing each other the best of luck, the two parted company and Pinocchio set off down the beach.

Not far from the place where he had fought with his schoolmates, Pinocchio met an old man walking along the sand.

"Pardon me, sir," he said. "Have you heard any news about the boy who was hurt here this morning?"

"No need to worry," said the old man. "He's all right."

"Then the wound wasn't serious?"

"No, but it might have been. Some rascal named Pinocchio threw a heavy book at him. What a good-for-nothing he must be!"

"That's not true!" said Pinocchio. "I know this Pinocchio well. He's a model boy—handsome, polite, kind to his father, an excellent student—" Suddenly Pinocchio realized that the old man was looking at him strangely. He glanced down at his nose. To his horror, he saw that it was growing longer by the second.

"Wait!" he cried. "Don't believe a word I've said. Pinocchio *is* a rascal—he's lazy, rude, unruly, and disobedient. In other words, the boy is a disgrace!" As soon as he said this, Pinocchio's nose returned to its normal size. Vowing to himself that he would never lie again, he said good-bye to the old man and continued on his way.

It was growing dark by the time he reached the Blue Fairy's cottage. Pinocchio hesitated before he knocked on the door. "How can I face my dear Blue Fairy?" he said to himself. "Will she ever forgive this last trick of mine? Perhaps she won't. And why should she? Oh, I am such a terrible rascal!" He grasped the knocker in his hand and then dropped it, losing courage. But just then lightning split the sky, there was a crack of thunder, and torrents of rain came pouring down. Pinocchio knocked on the door and waited. Half an hour went by, and then an hour. Soaking wet and shivering with cold, he knocked again. Another half hour went by. Then the top floor window opened and a large Snail wearing a nightcap peeked out. She was the Blue Fairy's maid, and she spoke very slowly. "Who is it?"

"Is the Fairy at home?"

There was a long pause. "The Fairy is asleep and must not be disturbed."

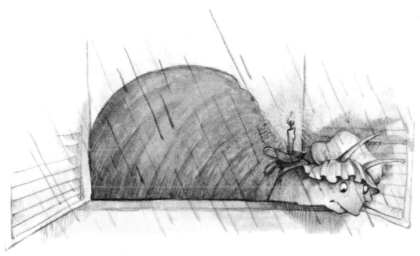

"Let me in, dear Snail. It's Pinocchio, and I'm dying of cold. Please hurry."

There was another long pause. "Wait for me there," came the Snail's voice. "But remember, I am a snail, and snails never hurry."

An hour passed, and then two hours. Pinocchio was so cold that his nose turned blue. He knocked on the door again. A window on the third floor opened and the Snail peeked out.

"Snail!" cried Pinocchio. "I've been waiting here for hours! Please hurry!"

There was a long silence. Then the Snail said, "Remember, dear boy—I am a snail, and snails never hurry," and the window closed.

A few minutes later midnight struck. Then it was one o'clock. Then two. And still the door did not open!

Finally Pinocchio lost all patience. He flew into a rage and kicked at the door so hard that his foot went through the wood and got stuck there. No matter how he squirmed and tugged, he could not pull it out.

Poor Pinocchio! For the rest of the night he stood at the door on one foot! When dawn came and the Snail finally appeared, he was so weak from pain and hunger that he fainted dead away.

When he woke up he was lying in his bed and the Blue Fairy was sitting next to him.

"Can you ever forgive me?" he whispered.

"Yes, I forgive you," she answered. "But you must not get into mischief again."

Pinocchio took her hand and swore that he would be good. And this time he kept his promise. He stayed out of mischief, studied hard, and at the end of the year he got the highest marks in his class.

The Blue Fairy was so pleased that she decided to give him a party.

"Tomorrow," she told him, "your dearest wish will come true. You will cease to be a puppet and become a real boy."

Pinocchio was overcome with joy. He even turned a somersault in delight! Then he rushed out of the Fairy's cottage to invite all his friends to the party. He visited one house, then another, until he had invited everyone but his favorite schoolmate, a boy called Candlewick. Candlewick had gotten his name because he was very tall and as thin as a string. He was also lazy and mischievous and had a wonderful imagination for pranks. Pinocchio admired him very much. Now he looked for him everywhere. Just as darkness fell, Pinocchio found him hiding by the side of the road that led out of the village.

"Candlewick! What are you doing here?"

"I'm running away," whispered his friend.

Pinocchio was horrified. "Don't do that!"

"You'd change your tune if you knew where I was going."

"What do you mean?"

"I mean I'm going straight to paradise," said Candlewick. "To a country where everyone plays all the time, where there are no books and no teachers, and where you can do exactly as you please from morning till night."

Pinocchio's eyes widened with curiosity. "What's this country called?"

"Playtime Land," said his friend. "Why don't you come along? You'd like it there."

"Oh, no," said Pinocchio. "I promised the Blue Fairy I'd be back before dark."

"What a pity!" said Candlewick. "Well, I'll think fond thoughts of you while I'm playing all day, staying up as late as I like, eating cake and candy . . . you'll be studying, of course."

"Of course," said Pinocchio a little sadly. "Well, good-bye, then."

"Stay just a little while," urged Candlewick. "The carriage will be coming soon, and you can see me off."

"I really should go," said Pinocchio, who was so tempted by Candlewick's description of Playtime Land that he could hardly move his feet. With enormous effort he started to walk off, but then he turned and asked, "Are you sure that there are no books and no teachers in Playtime Land?"

"None!"

"What about schools?"

"They've never heard of 'em!"

"So no one ever has to study?"

"NEVER!"

At this moment there was a soft jangling noise in the distance, and the faint sound of hoofs.

"It's the carriage!" cried Candlewick, jumping out into the middle of the road. And along came a brightly painted carriage drawn by six pairs of little gray donkeys. The carriage was filled top to bottom with boys of all ages.

"All aboard for Playtime Land," called the plump Coachman in a voice as sweet as candy. Candlewick scrambled onto the coach, pushing the other boys aside to make room for himself.

"And what about you, little darling?" the Coachman asked Pinocchio. "There's no room in the coach, but you can ride one of the donkeys."

"Pinocchio!" shouted Candlewick from inside. "Come with us and we'll always be happy!"

"We'll always be happy!" shouted the other boys, waving to Pinocchio from the coach windows.

The puppet did not know what to do. He stood there in the road with thoughts of games and toys and endless fun whirling through his head. Then, almost as if someone else were moving him, he suddenly found himself on the back of one of the little donkeys. All the boys cheered, the Coachman cracked his whip, and they were off.

Just as they broke into a brisk trot, the Donkey that Pinocchio was riding turned its head around and said, "Poor woodenhead! One day soon you'll cry bitter tears over what you've done tonight!"

A thrill of fear went through the puppet when he heard these words and saw tears shining in the Donkey's eyes. But they were moving along so quickly that he could not ask what the unhappy animal meant, or why it was crying. The road flew along beneath them, and soon they were inside the gates of Playtime Land.

Here Pinocchio's spirits lifted, for it was all he had been promised, and more. Everywhere he looked there were boys playing ball, chasing and tripping each other, riding bicycles, leaping, laughing, pushing, screaming, and having a rowdy good time. The noise was deafening, but Pinocchio thought it was wonderful. In no time at all he and Candlewick were as unkempt and dirty as the others, playing pranks, stuffing themselves with cookies and chocolates, staying up until all hours of the night, and congratulating themselves on how clever they had been to have come to Playtime Land.

Then one morning Pinocchio woke up, scratched his head, and felt something furry where his ear should have been. He rushed to the mirror and saw that he had sprouted a large, furry pair of donkey's ears! He pulled at them as hard as he could, but they only grew longer. He tried knocking his head against the wall, but that didn't help either. The puppet began to cry with shame. What had happened to him? Why had he left the Blue Fairy to run off with Candlewick? Deciding that Candlewick was to blame for all his troubles, Pinocchio made up his mind to find him and tell him so. But before he left his room, he pulled a long stocking cap over his ears to hide them.

The first person he met when he got outside was Candlewick. Strangely enough, he too was wearing a large stocking cap. "Why are you wearing that?" Pinocchio demanded.

"I hurt my foot, and the doctor told me to wear it," said Candlewick, blushing bright red. "And you, why are you wearing a cap, old friend?"

"Because I stubbed my toe." There was a moment of silence as the two friends looked at each other sheepishly. Finally Pinocchio said, "Tell me, have you had any pain in your ears lately?"

"Strange that you should mention it," said Candlewick. "They've been bothering me all morning."

"Mine too! Perhaps we have the same sickness. Why don't you let me see your ears?"

"I'll show you mine if you show me yours."

"I have an idea," said the puppet. "Let's take off our caps together. All right?"

"All right."

Up went their hands. At the count of one, two, three, the two friends pulled off their caps and threw them high into the air. At the sight of each other's donkey ears, they broke into helpless, astonished laughter and fell, rolling and kicking, to the floor. Then suddenly they began to bray just like donkeys. Worse, they discovered they

couldn't stand up. Instead they began to run and jump around the room on all fours. And as they ran their arms turned into legs, their faces grew into snouts, and their bodies sprouted long gray hairs. But the most horrible moment of all came when they each grew a tail.

"I won't be a donkey! I won't!" cried Pinocchio. But all that burst out of him was a loud "Hee-haw!"

Just then there was a knock on the door and the Coachman walked in carrying two bridles. "Good morning, my darlings," he said sweetly. "What fine little animals you've become. I'm here to take care of you." He bridled them, brushed them until their coats were smooth as silk, and then led them away to a market, where he put them up for sale. It was not long before a farmer bought Candlewick and a circus owner bought Pinocchio. The two friends were led off by their new owners in such haste that they could not even say good-bye to each other.

Once they were at the circus, Pinocchio's Master wasted no time in making himself clear: if Pinocchio did not do exactly as he was told, he would be rewarded with a painful crack of the whip. And so Pinocchio found himself eating dry straw and chopped-up hay and beginning his difficult training as a dancing circus donkey. Day after day he was forced to jump through hoops, to bow, to waltz and polka, and even to stand on his head.

Every time he made a mistake, his Master would shout that he was a jackass and beat him until he wept. Pinocchio's life at the circus was painful indeed, and he was very unhappy.

Then the day came when his Master decided that Pinocchio was ready to appear in public. A sign went up announcing his debut.

GALA PERFORMANCE TONIGHT!
PINOCCHIO, THE WORLD-FAMOUS DANCING DONKEY,
WILL MAKE HIS FIRST PUBLIC APPEARANCE!

That night the brightly lit circus tent was filled to overflowing with boys and girls who could not wait to see the new dancing donkey. And at last the moment arrived. The Master, wearing a red jacket, white breeches, and tall black boots, strode into the ring and announced, "Ladies and gentlemen! It is my honor and my privilege to present the greatest, the most famous, the most talented donkey in the entire world—the amazing Pinocchio!"

A fanfare sounded, the audience clapped and cheered, and Pinocchio was led into the ring. He looked splendid. His mane was braided with red silk tassels, his tail was woven with brilliantly colored ribbons, and a bright red harness jingling with brass bells hung around his neck. A gold and silver band gleamed at his waist, and flowers decorated his ears.

As Pinocchio reached the center of the ring the Circus Master cracked his whip. "Salute your audience!" he commanded.

Pinocchio bent his two front knees until he was kneeling, head bowed. The Master cracked his whip again. "Up!" he cried. Pinocchio rose up and began to prance around the ring—first slowly, then at a gallop. When he had circled it twice, the Circus Master pulled out a pistol and shot it into the air. The boys and girls screamed in surprise, and Pinocchio fell to the ground as if he were dead. The Master cracked his whip again and Pinocchio bounded up gaily, to a wave of excited applause.

As he began to pirouette around the ring, Pinocchio saw a woman who was strangely still and quiet in the audience of wildly cheering boys and girls. She wore a smile of terrible sadness, and soft blue curls fell to her shoulders from her bonnet. It was the Blue Fairy! Pinocchio stopped when he saw her and tried to cry out her name. But his cry of happiness was a long, comically loud "Hee-haw." The audience laughed, and the Circus Master, annoyed at Pinocchio's behavior, hit him on the nose with the handle of his whip. The blow was so painful that tears blinded Pinocchio's eyes.

When he could see again, the Fairy was gone. Poor Pinocchio! he

hung his head and wept bitterly. Then the Circus Master cracked his whip and commanded, "Now, jump through the hoop!" Though he tried, Pinocchio was so heartbroken that he passed under the hoop rather than through it. Enraged, the Circus Master cracked his whip once more, and Pinocchio tried again. This time he leaped high enough to pass through the hoop, but his hind legs got caught in it and he fell to the floor in a heap. When he managed to get to his feet, he was lame. Limping, and in great pain, he had to be led to his stall.

"There is no sense in keeping a lame donkey," said the Circus Master to the stable boy the next morning. "Take him away and sell him." The stable boy led Pinocchio to market, and before long he was bought by a village Musician. "This lame donkey has a good tough hide," said the Musician. "I can use it to make a drum for the town band."

The Musician headed for the rocky cliffs overlooking the ocean, for he planned to drown Pinocchio before skinning him. He tied a heavy stone and one end of a rope around Pinocchio's neck, kept tight hold of the other end, and pushed the donkey off the cliff into the deep water below. Down Pinocchio sank while the Musician sat at the edge of the cliff waiting for him to drown.

Several minutes went by. Certain that Pinocchio was dead by now, the Musician hoisted the rope up out of the water. He was speechless with surprise when he found, not a donkey, but a wooden puppet

with a long nose! "Where is my donkey?" he finally managed to sputter. "Have I been dreaming?"

Pinocchio smiled. "No, sir," he said. "I was the donkey that you pushed over the cliff. But while I was underwater, a school of fish swam along and began to eat me. They ate my furry ears, they ate my tail, and they kept on eating until they got right down to my wooden body. That was much too tough for them, so they gave up and swam away. And I am what is left—a puppet!" Laughing at the look of amazement on the Musician's face, Pinocchio dove off the cliff and swam away.

More determined than ever to find Geppetto, he swam steadily for most of the day. Suddenly he found himself approaching an enormous floating cavern. "Could it be an island?" he wondered. Drawing closer, he saw two huge rows of sharp yellow teeth and realized his mistake. It was not an island he was swimming toward, but the monstrous Dogfish! Pinocchio almost fainted with fright. He tried to swim away, but it was too late. The teeth loomed over him, the cavernous mouth opened wide, and Pinocchio was swept inside in a gulp as big and powerful as a tidal wave.

Then he was in inky darkness, trapped deep in the belly of the Dogfish. He would never see those he loved again! Grief-stricken, he began to wail and cry, until a quiet voice nearby said, "Courage!"

"Who's that?" asked Pinocchio, frozen with fear.

"A Tuna, swallowed when you were," said the voice. "And who are you?"

"A puppet, looking for my father. Can you tell me how to get out of here?" asked Pinocchio.

"There's no way out," said the Tuna glumly. "We'll just have to wait here until we're digested."

Just then Pinocchio noticed a tiny light flickering in the distance. "What's that?" he asked.

"I'm sure I don't know," said the Tuna. "Probably some other fellow waiting to be digested too."

"I'm going to find out," said Pinocchio. Groping and stumbling in the dark, he made his way toward the light until he came to its source. What he saw there made him blink with disbelief and then cry out with joy. Seated at a table lit by one flickering candle was an old man with a long white beard—Geppetto!

"Papa! Papa! Have I found you at last?" cried Pinocchio, rushing to embrace him.

"Pinocchio! My son! Is it really you?" Lifting him up, Geppetto covered his face with kisses, and the two of them broke into tears of happiness.

Then Pinocchio told Geppetto about all the adventures he had had since the day, so long ago, when Geppetto had sold his coat to buy Pinocchio a schoolbook. "Oh, my dear papa," he said, "how good you were to me, and what a bad son I have been to you! What troubles I have had since we parted! And how I have longed to find you!"

Geppetto held Pinocchio in his arms and told him how his little boat had capsized that stormy day at sea, and how the Dogfish had swallowed him, nearly two years ago.

"But how have you kept alive?" asked Pinocchio.

Geppetto explained that the Dogfish had also swallowed the cargo of a shipwreck—tinned food, candles, furniture, even blankets—and these had fed him and kept him warm inside the monster's belly. "But now," he sighed, "there is nothing left to eat, and when this last candle burns down, we will be in the dark."

"In that case, there is no time to lose," said Pinocchio. "We must escape! We'll go out the same way we came in, through the monster's mouth. Then we'll swim to safety."

"But I can't swim," protested Geppetto.

"I'll carry you on my back," said Pinocchio firmly. "I can swim well enough for two." Picking up the candle, he led Geppetto through the belly of the Dogfish and up its throat. From there they could see a patch of moonlit water and a bit of the starry sky, for the

Dogfish was sleeping with its mouth wide open.

"Now is the time," whispered Pinocchio, leading Geppetto into the Dogfish's mouth, across its long tongue, and over a row of its cruel yellow teeth. "Get on my back, hold on tight, and leave the rest to me," he whispered. Sensing Geppetto's fear, he added, "Don't worry, Papa, we shall soon be safe."

Geppetto climbed onto his back, and Pinocchio jumped bravely into the water. With a bright moon lighting the way, Pinocchio swam for miles, hopeful at first that land would soon come into view. But after many hours they seemed no closer to shore than when they had started, and the weight of Geppetto on his back made the puppet so weary that he could barely lift his arms and kick his legs. As his strength left him, he soon began to fear that he and his father were lost. As if reading his mind, Geppetto asked, "Are we going to drown, my son?"

Before Pinocchio could reply, a voice nearby said, "No one shall drown!" It was the Tuna that Pinocchio had met in the Dogfish's stomach, swimming alongside them. "Since you showed me the way out of the Dogfish, may I offer you a ride to shore?" he asked. Pinocchio and Geppetto accepted gratefully. They climbed onto his broad back and reached land in fine style as dawn was breaking.

After thanking him many times and patting him on his silver nose, they waved good-bye to the Tuna and set out on the road to town. Geppetto was so tired that he could hardly stand. Pinocchio helped him along, saying, "Lean on me, Papa. As soon as we come to a house I'll ask for some food and a place for you to rest."

They had gone no more than half a mile when they came upon two bedraggled creatures begging at the roadside.

One was a blind Cat dressed in filthy rags, and the other was a scrawny Fox who hobbled along with a rickety cane. Pinocchio saw that they were the two scoundrels who had tried to steal his gold coins from him.

They recognized him, too, and cried out pitifully, "Pinocchio!

Won't you come to the aid of two helpless creatures?"

"No, indeed," said Pinocchio. "You tricked me once, but you can't do it again."

"Believe me," whined the Fox, "we are truly poor and miserable."

"Poor and miserable," echoed the Cat.

"Then you deserve it," said Pinocchio. "Good day to you!" And with that he and Geppetto went on their way.

A bit farther down the road they came to a neat little cottage. As they walked inside Pinocchio called out, "Hello! Where is the master of the house?"

"Right here," came a familiar voice from the wall.

"It's the Talking Cricket!" gasped Pinocchio.

"Indeed it is, you little scamp," scolded the Cricket. "And don't suppose for a moment that I've forgotten how you threw that hammer at me!"

Pinocchio blushed with shame. "I'm sorry, Cricket," he said. "I know I deserve to be punished. Do with me what you will, but please be kind to my poor father."

"I will be kind to you both, for that is my nature," said the Cricket. "Stay here as long as you like," he told Pinocchio, "but mind your manners!"

Pinocchio thanked him politely and then asked, "How do you come to have such a fine house?"

"The Blue Fairy gave it to me. She left here in great sadness, believing that you had been eaten by that monstrous Dogfish."

"Will she come back?"

"I don't think so."

A wave of longing for the Blue Fairy swept over Pinocchio. But knowing that he should take care of his father right away, he fought back his tears and asked the Cricket where he might find some milk for Geppetto.

"There is a Farmer nearby who keeps cows. He will give you milk."

Pinocchio found the Farmer quickly and offered to work in exchange for the milk, since he had no money.

"That's fine with me," said the Farmer. "I need a good hard worker to draw water from my well."

Pinocchio started right away and didn't stop until he had drawn a hundred buckets of water for the Farmer's garden. When he finished, the Farmer paid him with a glass of milk, saying, "You've done as much work as my little donkey used to do. Poor beast, he's taken sick and now he's dying."

"May I see him?" asked Pinocchio. The Farmer led him to the barn. There in the straw lay a gaunt little donkey, so weak that it could no longer move. When Pinocchio looked into its eyes, he knew that he had found his friend Candlewick, and he wept over his schoolmate's unhappy fate.

From that day on, Pinocchio worked for the Farmer, drawing water, weaving baskets, and doing whatever he could to earn money to help Geppetto. He bought his father milk every day with his wages, and soon he had enough money for a little wagon, so that he could take Geppetto out for rides in the fresh air. After many months he even had some extra money, so he set off for the market one morning to buy himself a new suit of clothes.

As he skipped along the road he heard a voice ask very slowly, "Pinocchio! Do you remember me?" He turned to see the Snail who had been the Blue Fairy's maid.

"Of course I remember you!" said Pinocchio. "Tell me, how is the Blue Fairy?"

The Snail shook her head mournfully. "The Blue Fairy is very sick. She lies in her bed, too ill to see anyone, and now we no longer have money for food."

"Oh! My poor Fairy!" cried Pinocchio. He reached into his pockets and gave the Snail all his money, saying, "Take this, please. It's not much, but if you come back in a few days, I'll have more for her."

"Don't you need the money?"

"I was only going to buy some clothes for myself, and that's not important. Please—take it."

The Snail thanked Pinocchio and hurried off down the road with surprising speed.

Pinocchio went home and said nothing to Geppetto about giving his money away, for he didn't want to boast about his generosity. That night he wove baskets for many long hours so he could make extra money to give the Blue Fairy. Though the work made him weary, he didn't care. She had loved and trusted him, and his heart was set on helping her.

It was almost dawn when he went to sleep. As soon as he closed his eyes Pinocchio dreamed that the Blue Fairy was smiling down at him, her beautiful eyes shining with affection. She kissed him softly on the forehead, and he awoke.

On his bed he found a brand-new suit of clothes and a purse full of gold coins. There was a note inside the purse that said:

Bravo, Pinocchio! Your truly kind heart has made me proud of you. Accept these gifts in thanks from your Blue Fairy, and know that we will meet again soon. Before we do, your dearest wish will be granted.

Pinocchio tried on his new clothes and ran to the mirror. There he hardly recognized himself. Instead of the silly face, long nose, and rickety wooden arms and legs of a puppet, he saw a tall, dark-haired boy with bright blue eyes and a mouth that curved up at the corners. He was so overcome with surprise and delight that for a moment he wondered if he was still dreaming.

Then he ran into Geppetto's room and found another surprise. His father was in fine health once more and was happily carving a block of wood.

"Papa!" cried Pinocchio, throwing his arms around Geppetto's neck. "What has happened? How have all these wonderful things come about?"

Geppetto hugged Pinocchio. "All this is your reward," he said, "for bringing happiness to those who love you."

"And the old Pinocchio—where is he?"

Geppetto pointed to the corner where a wooden boy lay lifelessly against the wall, its head hanging down, its arms and legs sprawled out in different directions.

Pinocchio looked at the puppet for a long time. Then he said with great satisfaction, "How ridiculous I was when I was a puppet. And how glad I am to be a real boy at last!"

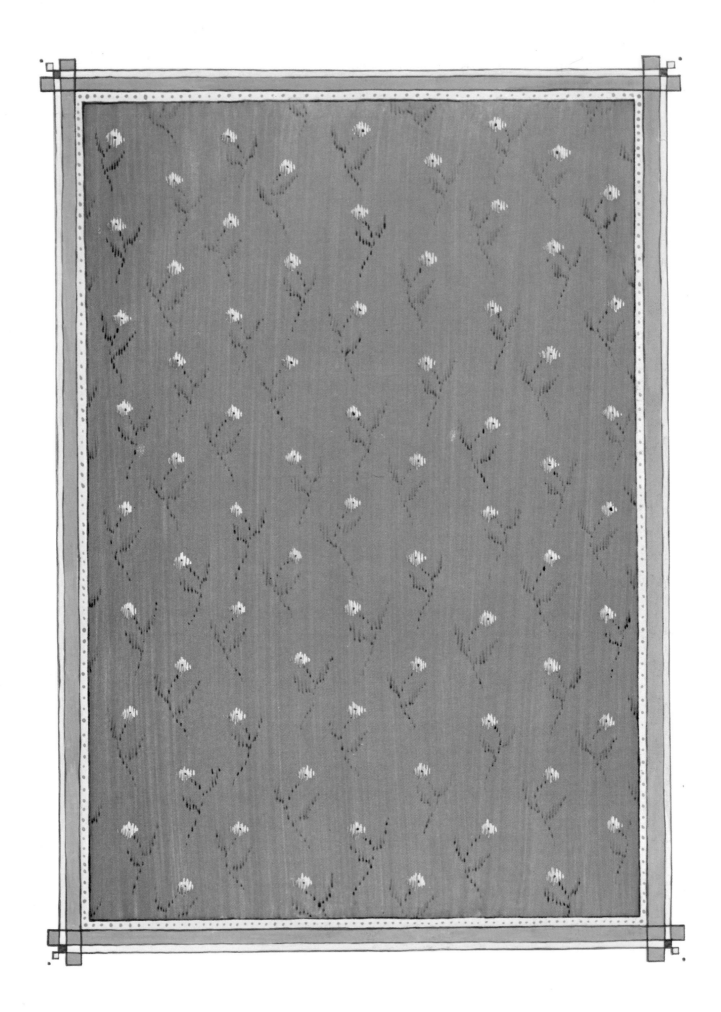